SPORTS SUPERSTARS

DREW BREES

By Kevin Frederickson

Kaleidoscope
Minneapolis, MN

Your Front Row Seat to the Games

This edition is co-published by agreement between Kaleidoscope and World Book, Inc.

Kaleidoscope Publishing, Inc.
6012 Blue Circle Drive
Minnetonka, MN 55343 U.S.A.

World Book, Inc.
180 North LaSalle St., Suite 900
Chicago IL 60601 U.S.A.

Kaleidoscope ISBNs
978-1-64519-037-0 (library bound)
978-1-64494-194-2 (paperback)
978-1-64519-138-4 (ebook)

World Book ISBN
978-0-7166-4340-1 (library bound)

Library of Congress Control Number
2019904590

Printed in the United States of America.

TABLE OF CONTENTS

Chapter 1: The First Super Bowl 4
Chapter 2: It Started with a Flag 10
Chapter 3: Lending a Hand 16
Chapter 4: Heading South 22

Beyond the Book 28
Research Ninja 29
Further Resources 30
Glossary 31
Index 32
Photo Credits 32
About the Author 32

CHAPTER 1

The First Super Bowl

Drew Brees takes the snap. A group of defenders runs toward him. Brees does not panic. He throws a soft pass. Running back Pierre Thomas catches it. Thomas runs 16 yards ahead. He is into the **end zone**. Touchdown! Brees celebrates with his teammates.

It is the third quarter of Super Bowl XLIV. It is the last game of the 2009 National Football League (NFL) season. The New Orleans Saints just scored. They now lead the Indianapolis Colts 13–10. This is the first time the Saints have played in the Super Bowl. Both the fans and the players are nervous. Brees tries to stay calm. The quarterback is a team leader. Brees hopes to lead the Saints to a title.

FUN FACT

In the 2009 season, Brees won three playoff games. The Saints won three playoff games from 1967–2008.

Drew Brees led the league with 34 touchdowns during the 2009 season.

The Saints fall behind in the third quarter. By the fourth quarter, the Colts lead 17–16. Brees crouches down. He yells out signals to his teammates. He steps back and throws a quick pass to the right. Tight end Jeremy Shockey catches it.

Shockey falls toward the end zone. A defender has his arms on Shockey. He tries to keep Shockey out of the end zone. But he can't. Shockey scores. The Saints take the lead!

FUN FACT

Drew Brees was *Sports Illustrated*'s Sportsman of the Year in 2010.

CAREER

STATS

Through the 2018 season

GAMES PLAYED	264
COMPLETIONS	6,586
PASSING YARDS	74,437
TOUCHDOWNS	520
INTERCEPTIONS	233

Brees holds up the championship trophy after winning Super Bowl XLIV.

But they have to hold on. Brees watches from the sidelines. He hopes his defense can finish the job. With 3:24 left, they seal the deal. Tracy Porter grabs an **interception**. He runs it back all the way. Touchdown! The Saints are going to win the Super Bowl.

It is time to celebrate. Brees takes the stage. The silver Super Bowl **trophy** is in his hands. He raises it high above his head. Confetti falls as he kisses it. The Saints are Super Bowl champions. And Brees led the way.

CHAPTER 2

It Started with a Flag

Drew Brees stood on a grass field. He was playing quarterback. But there were no pads. He just wore a belt over his clothes. Two yellow flags hung from the belt.

Drew was born on January 15, 1979. He grew up in Austin, Texas. Many kids grow up playing **tackle football**. But Drew played flag football. Tackling was not allowed.

Drew grew up in Austin, the capital of Texas.

There were no hard hits. His middle school did not have enough players for a tackle football team.

Flag football was good for him. He did not have to worry about being tackled. It was easy to work on his throwing and catching skills. He got good at passing.

Drew went to Westlake High School in Austin. There he played tackle football. He became the school's top quarterback. College coaches wanted Drew to come to their school. But then he got hurt in his second season.

College coaches stopped talking to Drew. He kept working hard. He came back for his last season. He led Westlake to an undefeated record. The team won the state championship. Drew was named the best offensive football player in Texas. It was a big honor.

Drew looks to pass for Westlake High School in 1996.

CAREER TIMELINE

1979

January 15, 1979
Drew Brees is born in Austin, Texas.

1996

December 1996
Brees leads his high school to the state championship.

1998

1998
Brees takes over as the full-time starter at Purdue University.

January 1, 2001
Brees plays his final college football game at the Rose Bowl in California.

2001

April 21, 2001
Brees is taken by the San Diego Chargers in the second round of the NFL **Draft**.

2001

November 4, 2001
Brees plays in his first game in the NFL against the Kansas City Chiefs.

2006

March 14, 2006
Brees signs with the New Orleans Saints.

2010

February 7, 2010
Brees leads the Saints to their first Super Bowl title.

October 8, 2018
Brees breaks Peyton Manning's record for most career passing yards.

2018

Drew set 19 school records while playing for Purdue.

No big colleges gave Drew a chance to play. They said he was too short. It was getting near the end of his senior year. Drew finally got an offer from Purdue University. It was a big school. But the school had not won much in football.

Drew changed that. He played four years at Purdue. His last year might have been the best. The Boilermakers beat top teams like Ohio State. Then, Drew helped Purdue get to the Rose Bowl. It's one of the best **bowl games** in college football. The Boilermakers hadn't been there in more than 30 years. It all changed with Drew as quarterback.

FUN FACT

Drew's dad played basketball in college at Texas A&M.

CHAPTER 3

Lending a Hand

Drew Brees stood on a street in New Orleans. He looked out. He saw damaged houses. People were living in trailers. Others were working on fixing their homes. Many people had left the city.

But Brees did not. He came to the New Orleans Saints in 2006. Hurricane Katrina hit New Orleans in 2005. The storm did a lot of damage. Brees tried to help **rebuild** the city.

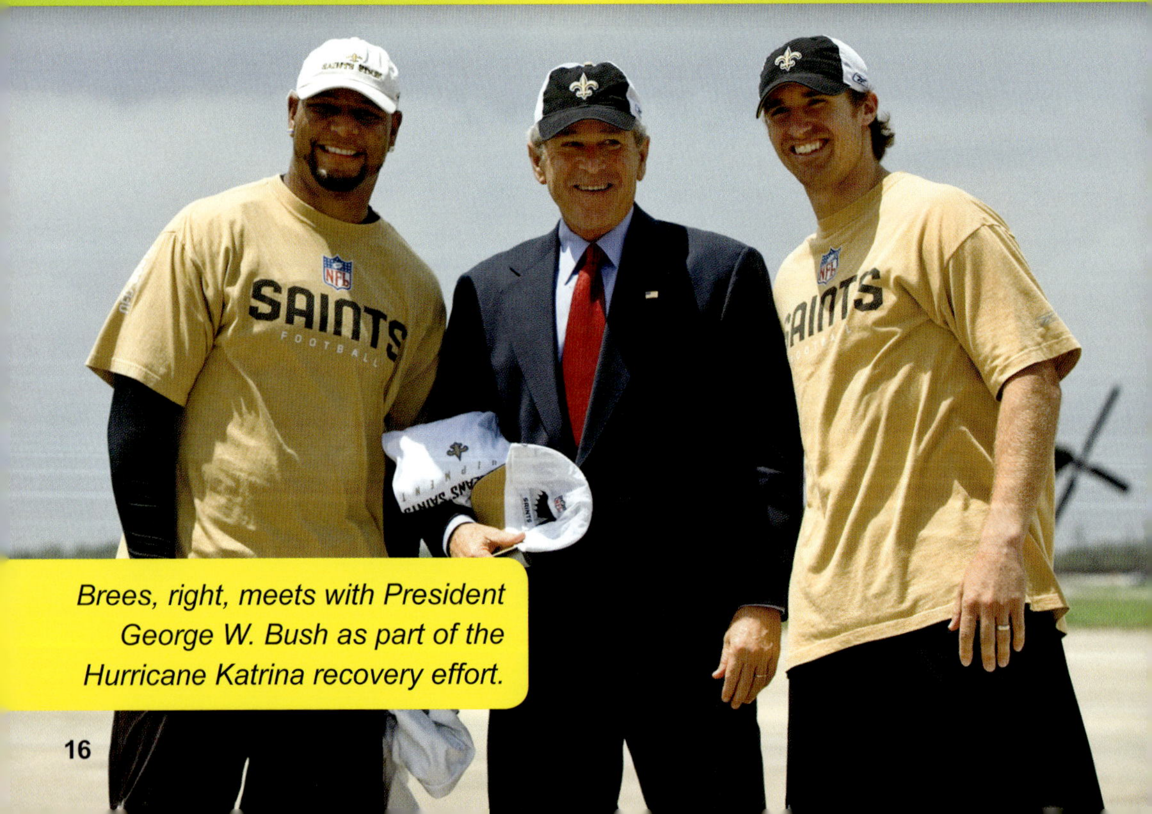

Brees, right, meets with President George W. Bush as part of the Hurricane Katrina recovery effort.

FUN FACT

Brees co-owns a restaurant in New Orleans called Walk-On's.

Brees tosses a football on a break with Katrina volunteers.

Brees helps rebuild homes in New Orleans in 2007.

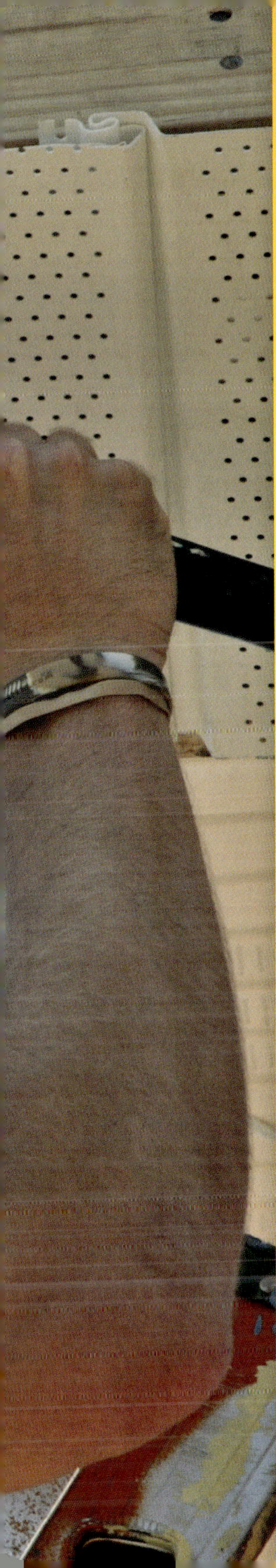

Other teams tried to sign Brees. But Brees chose the Saints. He saw how damaged the city was. But he did not care. He and his wife, Brittany, wanted to come and help. He spent time raising money for his charity. The charity was called Operation Kids: Rebuilding Dreams. They raised millions of dollars. The money helped build things for kids. They built schools and playgrounds.

Brees goes a long way to help. He has even traveled overseas. He believes in supporting the military. Two of his grandparents fought in World War II (1939–45). He visits military members serving in countries such as Iraq and Japan. He talks with the soldiers. He also takes pictures with them and signs autographs.

Brees has worked with First Lady Michelle Obama. They started working together in 2010. Brees and Obama want to help children be more physically fit. They want kids to eat healthy. They also want kids to exercise more.

Brees also spends time with his family. He has three sons and one daughter. They spend a lot of time together. Brees and his family also spend a lot of time at church. He goes to church nearly every week.

Now, Brees's sons play flag football. Brees coaches all three teams. He likes watching his kids succeed. He hopes they do what he did after playing flag football.

Where Brees Has Been

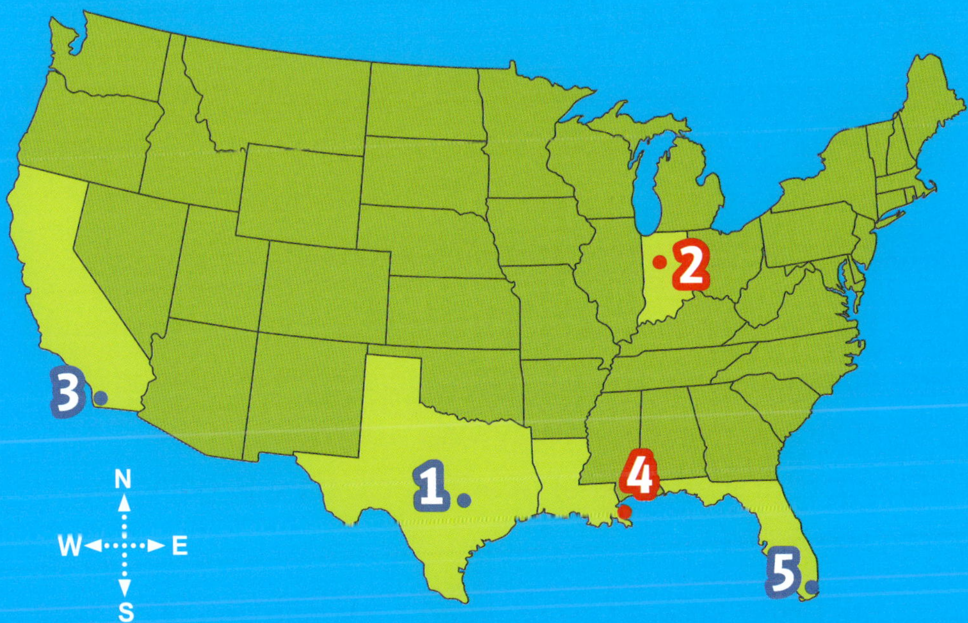

1 **Austin, Texas:** Where Brees was born and grew up.

2 **West Lafayette, Indiana:** Where Brees played college football at Purdue.

3 **San Diego, California:** Where Brees began his NFL career with the Chargers.

4 **New Orleans, Louisiana:** Where Brees plays with the Saints.

5 **Miami, Florida:** Brees and the Saints won their first Super Bowl here.

CHAPTER 4

Heading South

Brees started training for the 2001 NFL Draft. Teams had doubts about him. Some said he was too short. Others said his arm wasn't strong enough. Teams decided he wasn't good enough to be drafted in the first round.

The San Diego Chargers chose Brees in the second round of the draft. The Chargers were not a very good team. And Brees did not play very well. By 2004 the Chargers drafted another quarterback. He was going to replace Brees.

But Brees showed he could do it. He had one of his best seasons in 2004. He was named to the Pro Bowl. And he got the Chargers to the playoffs.

FUN FACT

Brees wears No. 9 because his childhood idol, baseball legend Ted Williams, wore the same number.

Brees threw for 12,348 yards as a Charger, the fifth most in team history.

Brees scrambles in his first home game as a Saint in 2006.

Brees played one more season in San Diego. During the last game of the season, Brees tried to pick up a fumble. He went for the ball. A defender landed on Brees. That caused him to injure his shoulder. He had to have major surgery. Some thought Brees might not play again.

The Chargers did not re-sign Brees. He almost went to play with the Miami Dolphins. But the Dolphins worried about his shoulder. Brees ended up going to New Orleans. The Saints had struggled in 2005. They hoped Brees could help turn things around.

PREGAME SPEECHES

In 2008, the Saints needed someone to give the team a pregame speech. Brees decided to do it. He became the player New Orleans went to for pregame speeches for many years after. He was very loud. He used positive messages. Players were ready to play after Brees's speeches.

Brees did that. He threw for more than 4,000 yards in his first season with the Saints. Then he helped New Orleans to its first Super Bowl in 2009. In 2018, Brees went up against the Washington Redskins. He threw a 62-yard touchdown pass. It was an important pass. Brees now had the NFL record for most passing yards by one quarterback.

Many people have doubted Brees during his career. But that hasn't stopped him. Brees has become one of the greatest quarterbacks in NFL history.

Saints fans hold up signs celebrating Brees breaking the NFL passing yards record in 2018.

Brees became the Saints' all-time passing yards leader in just his fifth season with the team.

BEYOND THE BOOK

After reading the book, it's time to think about what you learned. Try the following exercises to jumpstart your ideas.

THINK

THAT'S NEWS TO ME. The book talks about Hurricane Katrina hitting New Orleans. How might news sources be able to fill in more detail about this? What new information could you find in news articles? Where could you go to find those sources?

CREATE

PRIMARY SOURCES. A primary source is an original document, photograph, or interview. Make a list of different primary sources you might be able to find about Brees. What new information might you learn from these sources?

SHARE

SUM IT UP. Write one paragraph summarizing the important points from this book. Make sure it's in your own words. Don't just copy what is in the text. Share the paragraph with a classmate. What are your classmate's comments about the summary? Does he or she have additional questions about Brees?

GROW

REAL-LIFE RESEARCH. What places could you visit to learn more about Drew Brees? What other things could you learn while you were there?

RESEARCH NINJA

Visit www.ninjaresearcher.com/0370 to learn how to take your research skills and book report writing to the next level!

RESEARCH

DIGITAL LITERACY TOOLS

SEARCH LIKE A PRO

Learn about how to use search engines to find useful websites.

FACT OR FAKE?

Discover how you can tell a trusted website from an untrustworthy resource.

TEXT DETECTIVE

Explore how to zero in on the information you need most.

SHOW YOUR WORK

Research responsibly—learn how to cite sources.

WRITE

GET TO THE POINT

Learn how to express your main ideas.

PLAN OF ATTACK

Learn prewriting exercises and create an outline.

DOWNLOADABLE REPORT FORMS

Further Resources

BOOKS

Christopher, Matt. *Drew Brees*. Little, Brown and Company, 2015.

Kelley, K. C. *Top 10 Quarterbacks*. The Child's World, 2018.

Robinson, Tom. *Today's 12 Hottest NFL Superstars*. 12 Story Library, 2015.

WEBSITES

FACTSURFER

Factsurfer.com gives you a safe, fun way to find more information.

1. Go to www.factsurfer.com.
2. Enter "Drew Brees" into the search box and click .
3. Select your book cover to see a list of related websites.

Glossary

bowl games: Bowl games are postseason college football games. Purdue played in a bowl game in 2001 with Brees as quarterback.

draft: Sports teams use a draft to choose new players to play for them. Brees was chosen in the 2001 NFL Draft.

end zone: The end zone is where someone has to go to score a touchdown. Brees throws the ball to a wide receiver in the end zone.

interception: A pass that is thrown by one team and caught by a player on the opposing team is an interception. Brees missed his target and threw an interception.

rebuild: To rebuild is to put something back together. Brees helped the city of New Orleans rebuild after Hurricane Katrina.

tackle football: Tackle football is the traditional form of football in which players tackle each other. Brees didn't play tackle football until he was in high school.

trophy: A trophy is a prize or an award given to someone who has accomplished something. Brees held up the Super Bowl trophy.

Index

Austin, Texas, 10, 12, 13, 21

family, 19–20
flag football, 10–11, 20

height, 15, 22
Hurricane Katrina, 16

NFL Draft, 13, 22

Obama, Michelle, 20
Operation Kids: Rebuilding Dreams, 19

Pro Bowl, 22
Purdue Boilermakers, 13, 15, 21

Rose Bowl, 13, 15

San Diego Chargers, 13, 21, 22, 24–25
Super Bowl XLIV, 4, 6, 9, 13, 21, 26

tackle football, 10–12

Walk-On's, 17
Westlake High School, 12
Williams, Ted, 22

PHOTO CREDITS

The images in this book are reproduced through the courtesy of: Tom DiPace/AP Images, front cover (center), p. 7 (Drew Brees); Peter Read Miller/AP Images, front cover (right), p.3; EFKS/Shutterstock Images, front cover (stadium), front cover (field); Paul Spinelli/AP Images, pp. 4–5; Debby Wong/Shutterstock Images, p. 6; Red Line Editorial, pp. 7 (chart), 13 (timeline), 21; Paul Sancya/AP Images, p. 8; Jeff Bukowski/Shutterstock Images, pp. 9, 13 (helmet); CrackerClips Stock Media/Shutterstock Images, pp. 10–11; Ralph Barrera/Austin American Statesman/AP Images, p. 12; Jason Kolenda/Shutterstock Images, p. 13 (map); Scott Boehm/AP Images, pp. 14–15, 24; J. Scott Applewhite/AP Images, p. 16; Bill Haber/AP Images, pp. 17, 18–19; Shawn Pecor/Shutterstock Images, p. 20; Ted Sande/AP Images, p. 22; G. Newman Lowrance/AP Images, p. 23; David Goldman/AP Images, p. 25; Bill Feig/AP Images, p. 26; Mitch Gunn/Shutterstock Images, p. 27; dean bertoncelj/Shutterstock Images, p. 30.

ABOUT THE AUTHOR

Kevin Frederickson is a freelance writer and editor from Ohio. He lives near Cincinnati with his golden doodle, Max.